Mom

Goes

Shopping

by Michèle Dufresne

Pioneer Valley Educational Press, Inc.

Mom is going up.

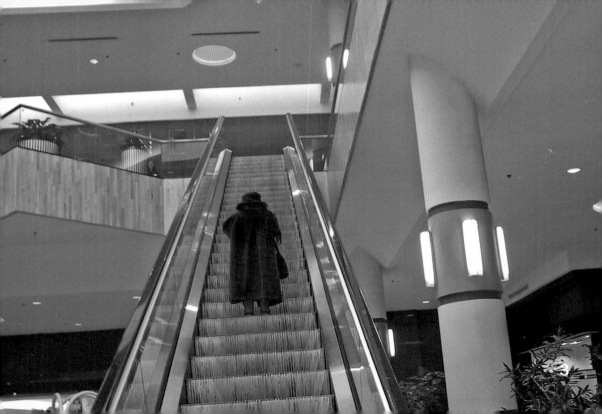

Mom is going down.

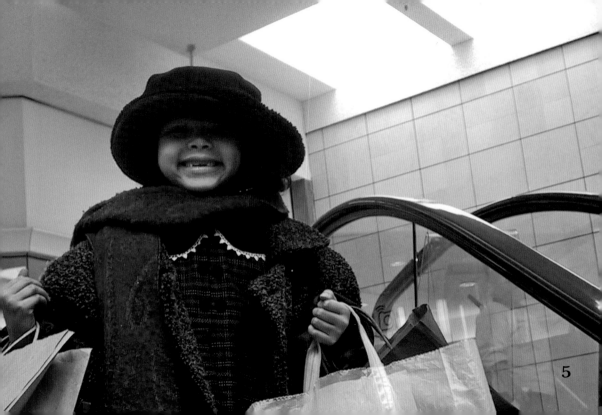

Mom is going up.

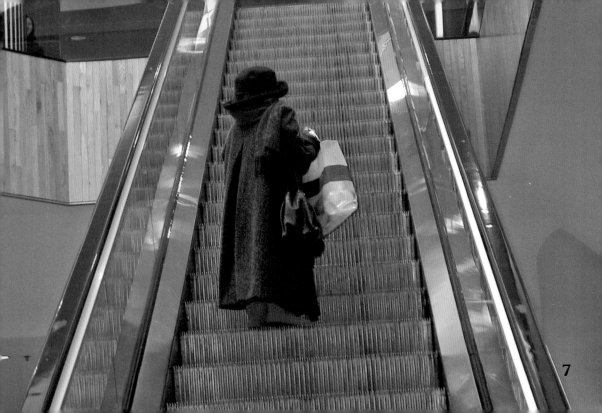

Mom is going down.

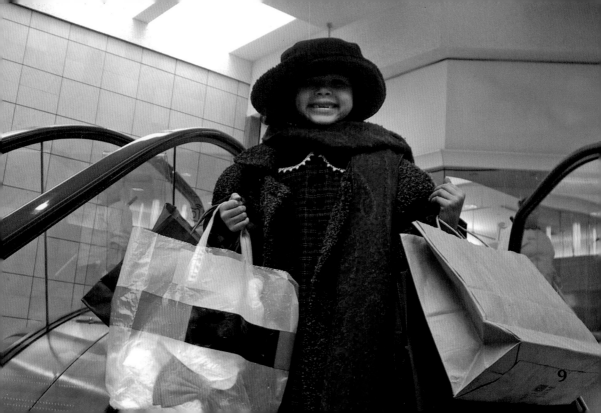

Mom is going up.

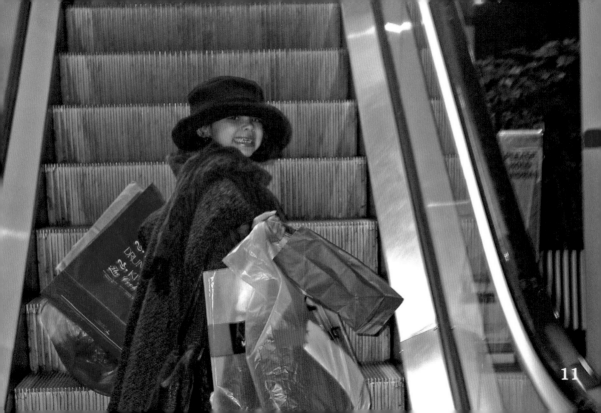

Mom is going down.

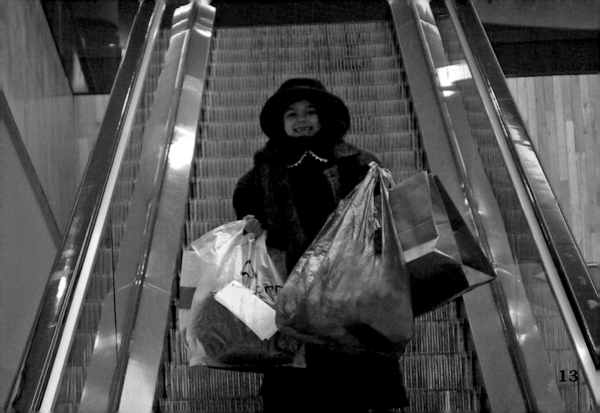

Mom is going up.

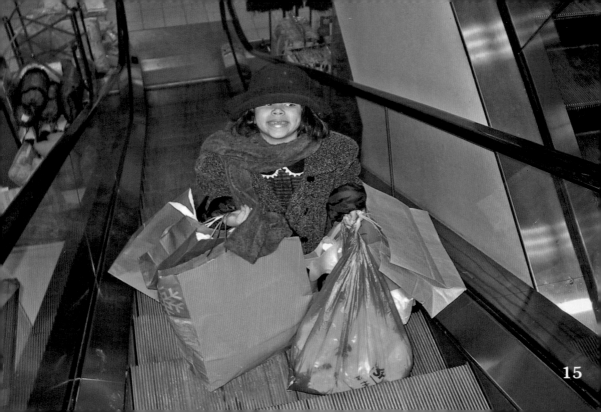
15

Mom is going down, down, down.

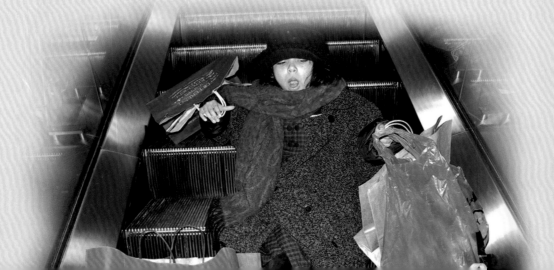